SHOCK
MONDAY

For my children, Duncan and Emily,
and for my father, whose memory I cherish.
G.B.

Thomas C. Lothian Pty Ltd
11 Munro Street, Port Melbourne, Victoria 3207

Text copyright © Gillian Bradshaw 1999
Illustrations copyright © David Cox 1999
First published 1999

National Library of Australia
Cataloguing-in-Publication data:

Bradshaw, Gillian, 1949– .
Shock Monday
ISBN 0 85091 866 9

I. Cox, David, 1933– . II. Title.

A823.3

Designed by Elizabeth Farlie
Colour separations by Color Gallery Sdn Bhd, Malaysia
Printed in Hong Kong by Wing King Tong Co Ltd

SHOCK MONDAY

Written by Gillian Bradshaw

Illustrated by David Cox

Lothian
B O O K S

Mum always drives me to school.

But this morning it was different.
I'd hardly opened my eyes when she said …
'We're walking to school today.'

'Is there something wrong with the car?' I asked.
'No. It's perfectly all right as far as I know.'

'But we've never walked before!' I protested.
'No time like the present, Tom.'

My little sister
Miriam danced
about.

Trust her.

'Breakfast done? Toilet?
Teeth cleaned? Hats on?
Off we go!'

Talk about the
morning rush hour.

Already Mum was taking great, loping strides,

with me dragging at the rear
and Miriam a yo-yo between us.

'Breathe the air,'
commanded Mum.
Really.
What did she think
we were breathing?

'Does anyone know why leaving the car
at home is a good idea?'
Who said it was a good idea?
'Well,' she said ...

'First, we save petrol,

which means we cut down on pollution,
but best of all ...

... walking exercises the heart and makes it stronger.'

She should have been a teacher.

I wondered if the heart grows weaker before it grows stronger as I staggered uphill under the weight of my schoolbag.

Then we caught up with another boy from school.
Mum slowed down to chat to his mum.

We got talking too,
and he said his
name was Wan Hing.

We saw things along the way
I'd never noticed when
we drove to school.
Like pale-headed
rosellas and
cuckoo shrikes,

real Remembrance Day poppies and shiny black seed pods that rattle. Miriam's pockets bulged with seed pods she'd collected. She looked like a bee with full pollen sacs.

Somehow my bag felt lighter.
Suddenly we were at
the school crossing.

'See you at lunchtime,' called Wan Hing.
'Right,' I said. 'Meet you on the oval.'

Our mums were sharing a joke behind us,
something about a shock on a Monday morning.
I could hear them laughing.

'We can walk to school every day,' I heard Mum
say, 'unless it's raining. And no protests, Tom.'

I kind of hoped tomorrow would be
fine, though I'd never tell Mum that.
It might lead to lentil sandwiches
or bird-seed cookies.
Who knows what she could do on
a health kick?

So I just said, 'Bye, Mum, bye, Miriam.
See you after school.'
Mum looked at
me happily.

I thought, 'No, no kisses.
My friends are around.'
You know how it is.

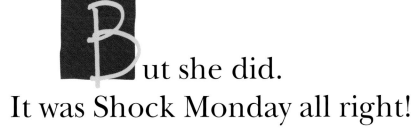ut she did.
It was Shock Monday all right!